# To Tell the Truth

by Patti Farmer
illustrated by Stephen Taylor

Stoddart Kids

*To Mike, who bought his way into this dedication*
*with his lasting loyalty, although the ten dollars worth*
*of bubble gum didn't hurt either . . .*
— P.F.

*Dedicated to all the people who made the book*
*possible and fun to do.*
— S.T.

Soddart Publishing gratefully acknowledges the support
of the Canada Council and the Ontario Arts Council
in the development of writing and publishing in Canada.

Published in Canada in 1997 by Stoddart Kids,
a division of Stoddart Publishing Co. Limited
34 Lesmill Road
Toronto, Canada M3B 2T6
Tel (416) 445-3333 Fax (416) 445-5967
e-mail Customer.Service@ccmailgw.genpub.com

Published in the United States in 1997 by Stoddart Kids
85 River Rock Drive, Suite 202
Buffalo, New York 14207
Toll free 1-800-805-1083
e-mail gdsinc@genpub.com

**Canadian Cataloguing in Publication Data**

Farmer, Patti
To tell the truth

ISBN 0-7737-3005-2

I. Taylor, Stephen, 1964–   II. Title.

PS8561.A727T6  1997   jC813'.54   C96-990026-0
PZ7.F23815To  1997

Printed and bound in Hong Kong

I am Benjamin Gates. I tell the truth.
And to tell you the truth, this has *not* been a good week.

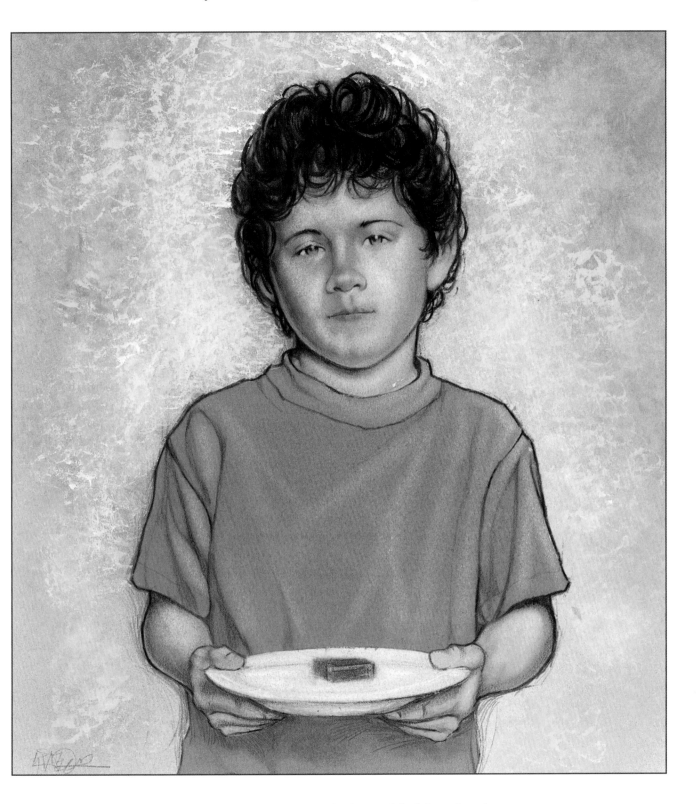

I stand here with my fudge, thinking back . . .

We are in art class. I am painting a rainbow.
I stand back and look. Pretty good, I think.
James O. looks, too. "Not bad," he says.

Then he shows me his. It is the dumbest rainbow
I have ever seen. He asks me what I think.
I tell the truth. "It's dumb," I say.

James O. paints another rainbow. This time on my face.
Everyone likes it. Except the teacher.
James O. is sent to the office. I am sent to the washroom.
"Nice rainbow," I call to him.

But James O. is not talking to me.

I go home after school. My mother is thrilled to see me.
I am still covered in paint. She hugs me anyway.

I tell her about my day.
She gives me apple juice and cookies.
"Tomorrow will be better," she says.

### *Tuesday, 2:30 p.m.*

Tuesday is not better.
The class is playing volleyball. I like volleyball.
But my team is losing. I watch the Tanner twins.
They take turns serving. The ball never goes over the net.

It is very clear. The Tanner twins are not tall enough.
"What are we doing wrong?" they ask.
I tell the truth. "You're too short," I say.

The Tanner twins seem a little upset.
They take turns bouncing volleyballs off my nose.
The teacher blows her whistle.
The Tanner twins have to do laps. I have to sit down.
"We can't all be good servers," I shout as they run by.

But the Tanner twins are not talking to me.

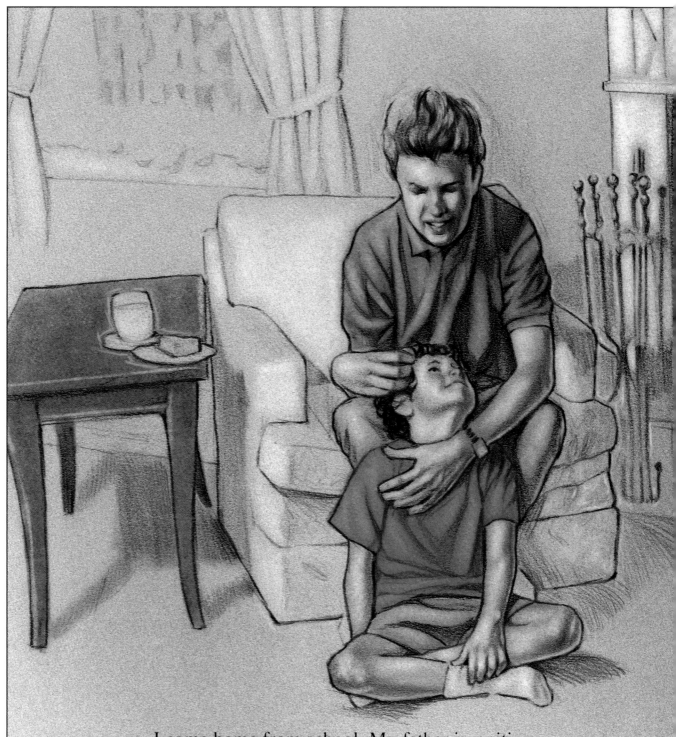

I come home from school. My father is waiting.
He wraps an arm around me. Then he ruffles my hair.

I tell him about my day.
He gives me milk and a piece of cake.
"Things will be better tomorrow," he says.

### *Wednesday, 10:44 a.m.*

It is morning recess, one minute before the bell.
Some of the guys and I are playing tag.
I am just about to tag a kid when
Melinda-May steps in the way. I miss the tag.

Melinda-May says she's sorry.
Then she says, "Do you like my new dress?"
Melinda-May is goofy. And so is her dress.
I tell the truth. "It's goofy," I say.

Well! Melinda-May decks me.
Suddenly I hear bells everywhere.
One in the school. A million more in my head.
Melinda-May is in trouble.
After class she picks up all the litter in the school yard.
I try to help. "You missed this," I say.

But Melinda-May is not talking to me.

I walk into the house.
My sister is watching T.V.
"Nice shiner, Benny," she says. "Have a doughnut."

I tell her about my day. "Don't worry," she says.
"It's not like the whole class has stopped talking to you."

***Thursday 9:00 a.m***.

Today is great. We're going to have a substitute teacher.
Everybody is laughing and talking.
Then the substitute teacher walks in and slams her ruler down.
"Who is making the noise?"

I'm still laughing. I tell the truth. "Everybody!" I say.

Everybody is writing, *I will not make noise.*
Two hundred times. In their journals.
I try to explain that I have to write it too.

Now the whole class *has* stopped talking to me.

My parents try to cheer me up.
"But no one is talking to me," I say.
"Telling the truth hurts."
My father smiles. "Sometimes it does," he says.

I turn to my mother. She nods in agreement.
She holds out a plate. "Fudge?" she asks.

I look at the fudge. It gives me an idea.

***Friday, 8:59 a.m.***

There I am with my fudge, ready to make peace.
The bell rings. I throw open the classroom door
and announce, "Fudge for everybody!"

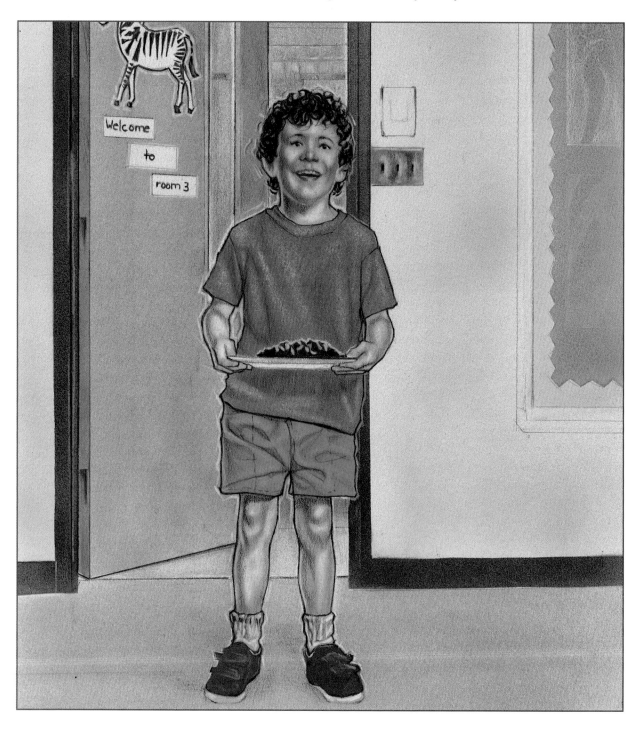

But no one cares.

At lunch I sit beside the Tanner twins.
I offer them some fudge.
They look at me. They look at my fudge.

They move to another table.

I slide next to Melinda-May.
I offer her a piece of fudge.

She folds her napkin. She folds her lunch bag.
She leaves without a word.

I am all alone. Just me and my fudge.
I think about James O. painting my face.
I think about the Tanner twins bopping my nose.
I think about Melinda-May making me hear bells.
Then I think about the whole class blaming *me* for telling the truth.

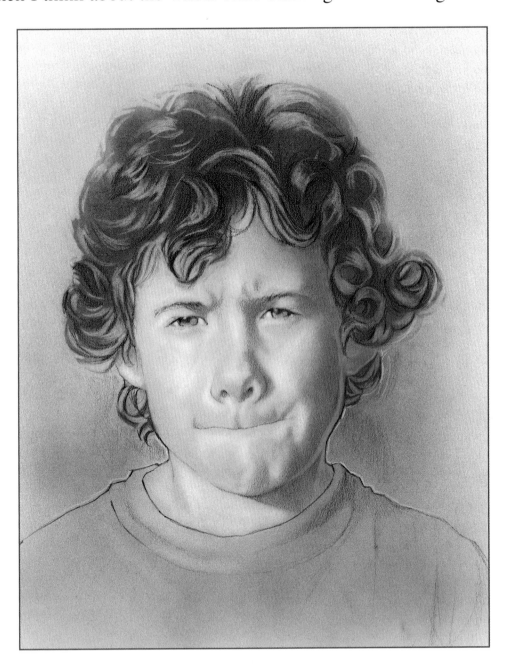

Now I am mad!

After lunch I march into class and yell,
"Who do you think you are?
You make me so mad I could spit!"

"There are rules against that," says the teacher.
"Take a seat Benjamin."
I take my seat.

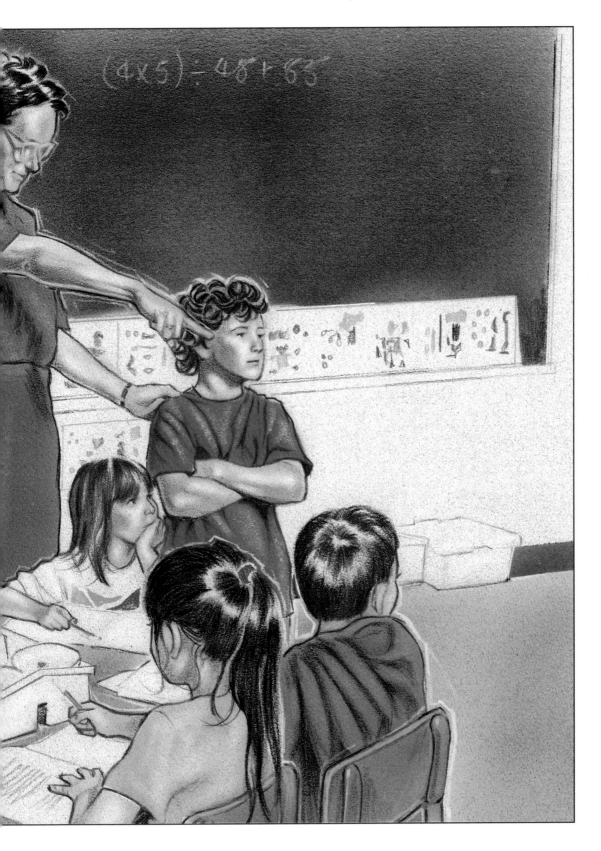

We are supposed to be reading.
James O. passes a note around the room.
Everybody reads it. Everybody signs it.

Then it is my turn. I open the note. It says:
*BENJAMIN GATES IS A BIG JERK!!!!*
*Sign here.* _____

And it is signed by the whole class.

Suddenly the teacher looks up.
"Who is passing notes?" she shouts. "Do *you* know, Benjamin?"
The whole class freezes. There is panic in their eyes.
I have them where I want them. I tell the truth. "Yes," I say.

I pass the note back and forth in my hands.
"I am."
Then I chew up the note and swallow it.
A giant sigh fills the room.

After school I write, *I will not pass notes.*
Five hundred times. On the blackboard.
I could be here forever.
But to tell you the truth, I do not mind.

I know my friends are waiting for me.
The whole class. Outside.
Eating my fudge . . .

. . . and saving a piece for me.